This book belongs to

.............................................

For Mark 'The Claw' Shaw – D.O.

For Arlo, Elsa and Finn – P.B.

This edition published in the UK in 2019 by Scholastic Children's Books
Euston House, 24 Eversholt Street
London NW1 1DB, UK
A division of Scholastic Ltd
www.scholastic.co.uk
London ~ New York ~ Toronto ~ Sydney ~ Auckland
Mexico City ~ New Delhi ~ Hong Kong

First published in 2017 by Scholastic New Zealand Ltd.

Text copyright © Dean O'Brien, 2017
Illustrations copyright © Paul Beavis, 2017

ISBN 978 1407 19659 6

# Stink-o-saurus

Written by
## Deano Yipadee

Illustrations by
## Paul Beavis

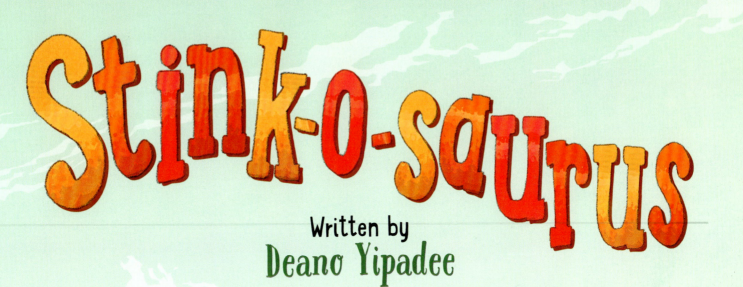

Long, long ago,
when dinosaurs roamed the land,
there lived a tiny little one,
whose name was Stan.

He was a rare dinosaur,
a one of a kind.
Most **roared** from their front,

his **roar** came from his behind!

When Stan asked others
to join him and play,
they groaned,
**"Not today, Stan.
Go away!"**

It was his rear-end roar
that caused such a fuss
because Stan was the very first
stink-o-saurus.

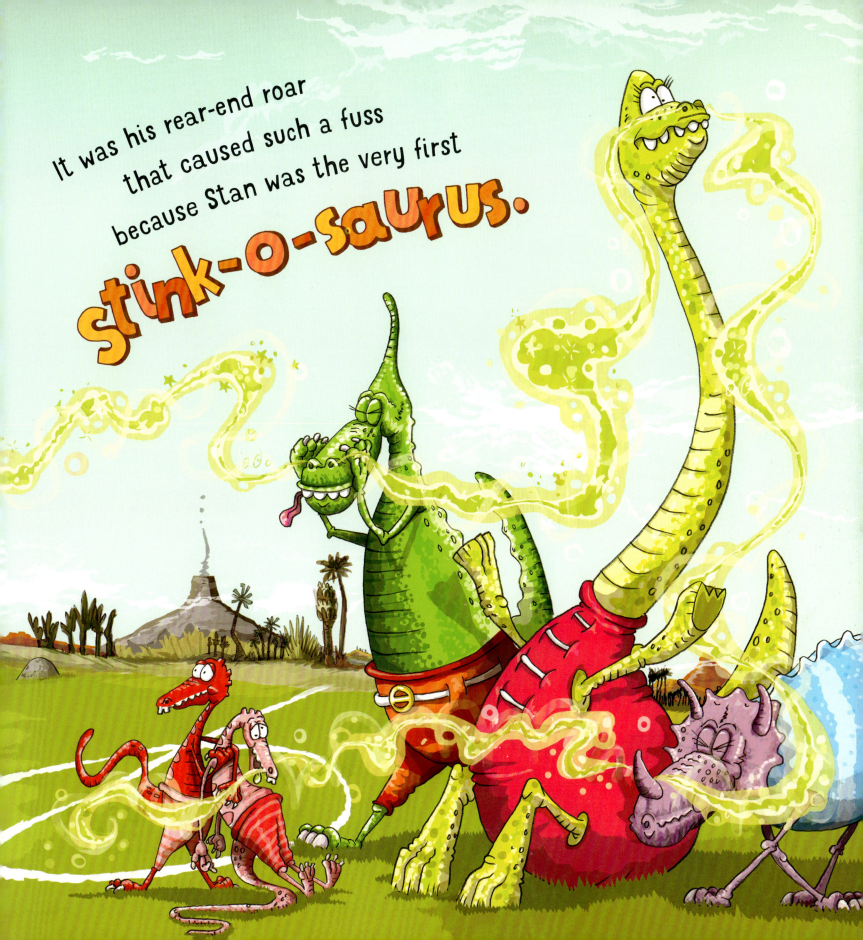

So he walked into the jungle,
going STOMP,
STOMP, STOMP,

eating over-ripe bananas,
with a CHOMP,
CHOMP,
CHOMP.

They caused
a **rumble**
from his tum,
then a sound
from his bum!

It was a noise so loud,
then out came a

WHIFFY CLOUD!

One day, Tommy T-Rex thumped into town,
**gobbling** up clean laundry and **kicking** houses down!

Tommy **snatched** all the candy
as the dino children cried.
Whenever he came along,
every dinosaur would hide.

As Tommy **munched** their goodies,
he heard a noise in the trees.

He found Stan eating 'nanas...

and

ROARED

him to his knees!

Startled and afraid,
Stan hid his eyes with his hands,

and his
small legs
started
**shaking**
in his
Stink-o-saurus
pants.

Stan tried to run fast, going

STOMP, STOMP, STOMP.

Tommy laughed behind him, going

CHOMP, CHOMP, CHOMP.

Stan leapt
behind a tree
and shrieked,
"Get away
from me!"

But as Tommy circled round,
Stan sank down to the ground.

He hid his head
between his legs,
his tail **FROZE**
in fear ...

That's when out
**BOOMED**
that funky flame,

knocking T-Rex

on his rear!

P-F-F-F-F-F-F-t!

Forget about King Kong,
Tommy was flattened by King PONG!
And as he clambered to his toes,
that stink went straight into his nose.

That shaken T-Rex was so big,
but his arms were very small.
In fact, he couldn't reach his nose
to block the smell at all!

He **spluttered** and he **wobbled**
as the land began to shake,

because
Stan the Stink-o-saurus
had caused the first

EARTHQUAKE!

So Tommy T-Rex ran away,
going

**THUMP, THUMP, THUMP.**

Stan the hero ran behind him,
going

**TRUMP,
TRUMP,
TRUMP!**

The dinosaurs danced and hollered,

"Hip-hip HOORAY!"

for that little Stink-o-saurus
had gone and saved the day.

Some say it was an Ice Age that made dinosaurs extinct. Was Earth struck by a comet? Or hit by a BIG STINK?

But there's a chance that Stan survived ... and hides ... in your underpants!

I think that I can smell him when your noisy bottom rants...

P-f-f-f-f-f-f-f-t!

stink-o-saurus!